THE Wuzzolympics

Adapted by Wade Wallace
Based on an episode by Frederick Stroppel

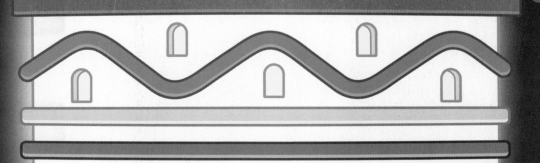

SCHOLASTIC INC.
New York   Toronto   London   Auckland   Sydney
Mexico City   New Delhi   Hong Kong

ISBN: 978-0-545-20666-2

Based on the TV series *Wow! Wow! Wubbzy!* as seen on Nick Jr.®, created by Bob Boyle.

www.wubbzy.com

12 11 10 9 8 7 6 5 4 3 2 1   10 11 12 13 14 15/0

Printed in the U.S.A.   40

First printing, January 2010

"Wow, wow!" said Wubbzy. "It's time for the Wuzzolympics! Michelle Kwanzleberry is the coach this year. She's the most famous Wuzzolympic athlete of all time!"

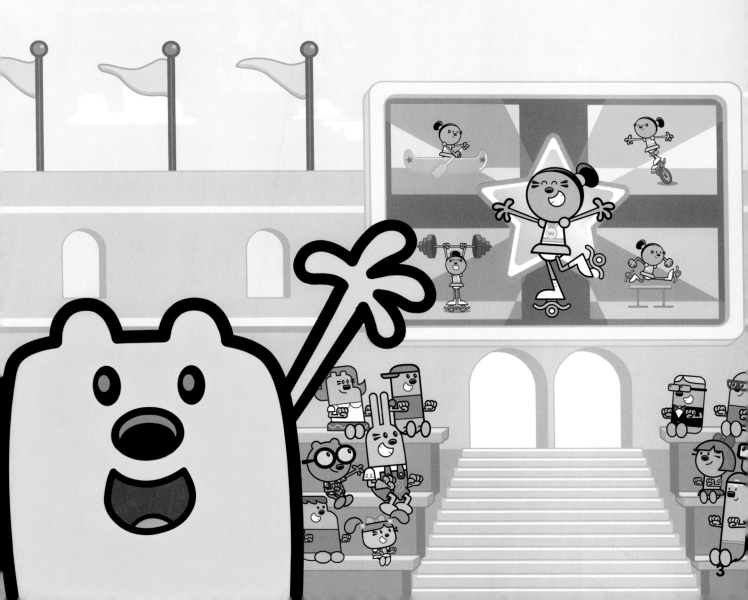

"I can't wait to race in the Wuzzleburg Wacky Dash," Wubbzy told Michelle. "I want to win!"

"The three most important things in sports are *prepare*, *practice*, and *have fun*," said Michelle. "If it's done with fun, you've already won!"

"Oh, I don't need to practice," said Wubbzy. "With this spring, my tail has twice as much bounce as before."

Then Michelle went to see Widget.

"Widget, are you preparing and practicing for the race?" asked Michelle.

"Oh no," said Widget. "I reckon I can win this race with my Jiffy-Jogger 3000."

Next Michelle stopped by to see Walden.

"Walden, are you preparing and practicing for the race?" Michelle asked.

"I don't need to," said Walden. "With my fancy outfit, I can win the race by calculating the wind currents!"

Later that day, Michelle visited Daizy.

"Daizy, are you preparing and practicing for the race?" Michelle asked.

"I sure am!" chirped Daizy. "I've been studying the map and practicing my running and skipping! It doesn't matter if I win or lose, I'm just going to have fun," she sang.

"Good work, Daizy!" cheered Michelle.

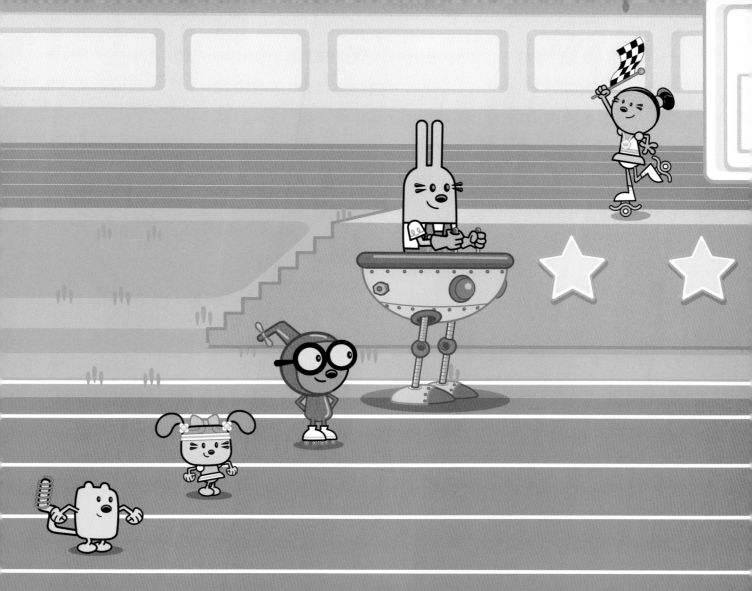

Finally it was time for the Wuzzleburg Wacky Dash.
"Wacky Dashers," called Michelle. "On your mark, get set, go!"
The race was on!

First the racers came to the Great Wall of Wuzzle.
Whoosh! Walden flew over it using his wings.
Boing! Wubbzy bounced over it.

WHOOSH!

Widget was speeding toward the Great Wall when the Jiffy-Jogger 3000 went out of control!

"Whoa!" she cried as the machine threw her into a bush.

"La la la la!" sang Daizy. When she came to the wall, she pulled out her map. "The Great Wall has a staircase I can use!"

At the Soupy Swamp, Walden was sailing into the lead. "This race is a breeze!" he said.

But then a gust of wind blew him down into the icky water! When Daizy came to the Soupy Swamp, she remembered that she had practiced her skipping. She skipped across the stones easily.

SPROING!

"I'm winning!" Wubbzy shouted at the Bendy Bridge over Goofy Gulch.

"With my springy tail, I can save time by bouncing right over the bridge!" cried Wubbzy.

Wubbzy was high in the air when he accidentally landed on a Pizza-Eating-Bo-Bo-Bird — flying the wrong way!

Meanwhile, Daizy slid down the Bendy Bridge!
"*Wheeeeeee!*" she shouted. "This is so much fun!"

Back at the Wuzzolympic Coliseum, Michelle and the rest
of Wuzzleburg waited at the finish line.

"Here comes the first Wacky Dasher now,"
Michelle called. "And it's . . . Daizy!"

Then Wubbzy, Widget, Walden, and the other Wacky Dashers raced into the coliseum.

"Wow, wow! Daizy, you won the Wacky Dash,"
cheered Wubbzy.
"She did all the right things," said Michelle.
"Daizy prepared, practiced, and had fun!"

The crowd cheered as Daizy received her Wuzzolympic medal. "Congratulations to everyone who played in the games," said Michelle Kwanzleberry. "Remember, if it's done with fun, you've already won!"